CLUE IN THE HEIRLOOM

CLUE IN THE HEIRLOOM

ARYAN GUPTA

MP
MAHAVEER PUBLISHERS

Published by
MAHAVEER PUBLISHERS
4675/A, Second Floor, 21-Ansari Road,
Daryaganj, New Delhi – 110002
Ph. : 011 – 66629669–79–89
e-mail : mahaveerpublishers@gmail.com
website : www.bookpremi.com

First Edition : September 2014

Clue In The Heirloom
ISBN(10) : 9350880989
ISBN(13) : 9789350880982

This novel is entirely a work of fiction. Names, characters and incidents portrayed in it are the work of the author's imagination. Any resemblance to actual persons, living or dead, events or localities is entirely coincidental.

Distributed in India by
VAIBHAV BOOK SERVICE
e-mail : vaibhavbookservice@gmail.com

Distributed in Nepal by
BAJRANGBALI BOOK ENTERPRISES PVT. LTD.
Jyatha Mushyabahal, Ward No. 27, Kathmandu, Nepal
e-mail : bajrangbalibooks@gmail.com

Printed in India

Dedicated to My Dear Sister
Muskan Gupta

Acknowledgments

Few years back, I hated books. But seeing my sister read them with so much interest, I soon developed a habit of reading. If it was not for my sister, Muskan I would never have been able to write this book.

I would also like to thank my cousin sister, Devanshi inspired by whom I took a pen and paper and decided to try out my hand in writing. Initially I found it boring and tough. My first attempt was unsuccessful and I failed. Again, I tried and this time, new ideas kept coming to me.

This book is the result of my hard work and constant encouragement from my loving family and friends.

I would like to thank my father for his constant motivation and my mother for always being curious to know the developments in the book. They constantly supported me and were a comfort during long hours when I didn't know what to write. My mother helped me balance between my studies and sports giving me immense support and valuable time for writing this book.

I would also like to mention my grandparents without whom this book would not have made it and quite possibly, I would have failed to write this book. They were a constant source of strength to me.

I would also like to convey my special thanks to my phoophaji Mr. Atul Bansal, Pradeep uncle and Mahaveer Publishers, for without their support this book would not be in the hands of my readers.

I would like to convey my heartfelt thanks to all those who helped me while I wrote this book and hope my readers will find this book captivating.

Contents

1

A Strange Mystery

“What a marvelous show!” said Rohan to his brother Akash Malhotra as they sat in their classic white BMW after watching the famous show Zangoora in Kingdom of Dreams, Gurgoan. Rohan and Akash were both good–looking teenagers of eighteen. “The Culture Gali was perfect,” Akash remarked. “The best part of the Culture Gali was the beachside of Goa”. “Yeah! I would have liked to throw you in the sand.” Rohan teased. As their house came into view, they slowed their car and then parked it. “Hi Dad!” said Rohan as they entered the hall. Their father, Amar Malhotra, was a well known police inspector. He had solved many cases and wanted his sons to be like him. “Hi!” he said in his calm voice. “Are you working on a case?” Akash asked curiously.

"Well not at the moment," said Mr. Malhotra. "Gurgaon seems very peaceful nowadays. Anyways, have you heard of our new neighbor, Miss Simon Roll. She is from London. She is a very lavish lady. The treasures she owns, you must see them."

"Wow! Sounds interesting," said Akash with a twinkle in his eyes. "I'd like to see her."

They were now heading to the dining room where Tara Malhotra and the housekeeper, Miss Sharma were arranging food on the table. After eating, the boys went up to their bedrooms and slept soundly.

In the morning, as the boys came down for the breakfast, a young lady was standing in front of them. She was looking like a Queen. She wore such expensive clothes. She also looked like a British woman. Just then, their mother entered the room and introduced the woman. "Rohan, Akash, she is Miss Simon Roll, our new neighbor. She is here because I invited her for breakfast. Now, I must hurry to the kitchen. You two have a chat with her as she wants to speak to you. Till then, I will prepare breakfast with Rita, the housekeeper." Saying this, she scurried off to the kitchen.

The boys wondered that they had never met Miss Roll, then why would she want to speak to them? The question was immediately answered "Ah! So you two are the sons of Mr. Malhotra," She said in a British accent. "I have heard a lot about you from your father. He says you helped him in some cases. Well, I want some help too, if you please?"

"You bet!" said the boys happily. At last, there will be a case they are going to handle together. They smiled. Both had the same thought in their minds, "What's the mystery about? Is the mystery a normal one or needs to be handled by some intelligent brains." They were very excited and looked eagerly at Miss Roll.

"My story starts from here. Many years ago, my father, brother and I lived in a wealthy mansion. My father was a grand sailor. He travelled great distance, and always brought treasures with him. His business flourished and we were happy. But then slowly he became old. He did not sail anymore for fulfilling our needs. We sold some treasures. Then my younger brother became a sailor but he did not bring treasure every time he went. Then one day he brought the greatest treasure ever known to the world. He brought an antique piece of jewellery made by the finest craftsmen of that time. It was worth billions and billions of pounds. It was the best piece of jewelry I ever saw. Even though we needed money we didn't sell it. It became the heirloom of the family. Then my brother went to another venture. This time he came to India. But before coming to India, he summoned a craftsman and told him to cut the heirloom in half! I was amazed to hear that. Then before coming here he gave me one half of the heirloom and took the other half of it and then he said, "If I don't return in six months, with the help of it, you can find me. And then he left."

There was an awkward silence after this little speech. The silence was broken by Akash. He asked, "By it, did he mean the heirloom?" "Yes," said Miss Roll, weeping. "Can we have a look at your brother's photo and the heirloom?" asked Rohan hopefully. "Yes," she said again. "You can come tomorrow at my house around ten," saying this she wiped her eyes.

Rohan was about to ask something but suddenly Mrs. Malhotra and Miss Sharma came out of the kitchen and started setting the breakfast on the table. Mr. Malhotra also came out of his study room. As soon as the boys saw him, they decided to discuss the matter with him. Till then they behaved as if nothing has happened. "Wow! Boiled eggs, ham sandwiches with jam and cheese! What could be better

Rita?" remarked Rohan with a pleased look at the housekeeper.

The rest of the day was uneventful. At night, Rohan and Akash went to their father to discuss about the mystery, who added his thoughts about it, "Well, I don't know how you can find Miss Roll's brother for this is certainly a very 'Strange Mystery." "Yeah! It seems impossible to find her brother with no clues to start with," said Akash and they all went to bed.

2

The Heirloom – and a Fatal Attack

The next morning, the boys were very excited about the heirloom, so they got up early in the morning and had a 'simply fab' breakfast as Akash called it. At quarter to ten they went to Miss Rolls' mansion and stared at it in awe.

The windows were carved skillfully and looked beautiful with the silk curtains placed inside which they were able to catch a glimpse of. The whole mansion was covered with artificial yellow and green ivy and was surrounded with a pleasant and colorful garden.

When they reached the doorstep, they found out that there was a knocker. They pulled it, and waited for several minutes but nobody came out. They became worried.

"I am sure something has happened to Miss Roll," said Rohan anxiously.

"I'll check the grounds," offered Akash.

He did a thorough search but could find nothing. When he reached the back door, he stopped. He heard a male voice, but there was no one in the house. He covetously hid behind a bush.

The back door swung open and two men came out.

They were really different from each other, but Indians. One was a short slender person with a crooked nose and a circle scar on his right cheek. The other man was tall, burly man. He had an extra finger on his left hand. The first man had a huge packet which he thought was Miss Rolls' treasure and he guessed right as the second man said in his bold voice. "Aman, take the heirloom and get to the car while I buy a bag to put it in."

"Yes boss," said Aman.

"Oh! So they are stealing the heirloom," thought Akash. He acted quickly. As soon as the burly figure had gone, he came out of his hiding and struggled for the packet. He took the packet from the man but couldn't catch him, still he was happy that the heirloom was safe. Rohan heard all the commotion and came to the back door. When he heard of the recent happenings, he sighed.

"Thank God! The heirloom is safe." Then Akash suddenly said, "My God I forgot. Something must have happened to Miss Roll." With that he broke into the house from the rear door, closely followed by Rohan.

They were not surprised to see almost everything upside down or broken. The thieves had broken most of the treasures and also broke the glass case where the heirloom was kept. "But why did they break the other things if they took only this?" questioned Rohan, pointing at the package. "Perhaps they tried to find the key to the case but could not find it so, broke it ." said Akash. Then suddenly they heard muffled cries coming from upstairs. They ran for it. The voice was coming from the attic. They broke in and saw a figure. Bound and gagged lay Miss Roll! "What!" said the two voices.

Miss Simon Roll lay unconscious on the floor. The boys were terrified. They checked her pulse. She was alive!

They helped her regain consciousness. She slowly and gradually sat up, her forehead aching. "Tha-Thanks," she said in a croaky voice. Her face was ash white and she looked very disturbed and weak. Akash helped her to reach her room. She was very scared. When they reached her room, they were alarmed. Miss Roll was shouting, "Crooks! Crooks! Where are they?" "They are gone," said Rohan.

"Gone? Oh no. There were so many valuable and ancient treasures displayed. They should not be stolen.

"No, they're not," said Rohan, "We came here in time to save..." "Did they take away the necklace?" Miss Roll broke in. "What necklace are you talking about," asked Rohan anxiously. "There wasn't any necklace downstairs."

"Oh! I mean my heirloom."

"Is it a necklace? Well it is perfectly safe." Rohan assured her. He narrated the whole incident to her with some 'Ooo's' and 'Wow's' from Miss Roll.

"Oh! How can I thank you? You boys are so brave." Miss Roll said after Rohan finished.

"But there is one thing that I do not understand," said Akash looking inquiringly at Miss Roll, "Is that why those funny looking thieves stole only the necklace? If it had been just a simple robbery, they would have taken almost everything valuable from this house."

"Yes! I just don't see any point in that!" said Miss Roll

"But I think I do!" said Rohan brightening up quite suddenly. Both of them (Akash and Miss Roll) were surprised but anxious for him to go on.

"Miss Roll, do you remember that what your brother said after giving the heirloom to you?" "Yes," said Miss Roll. "He said that if he doesn't return in six months, with the help of the heirloom I could find him."

"Yes and it's been nine months and I think he's kidnapped for some reason." Miss Roll said.

"Yeah! And I have a hunch that those kidnappers got to know what your brother said and were trying to steal the heirloom so that you couldn't find out the secret." finished Rohan.

"Well, I think this rings a bell." Akash remarked.

"Of course it does. It is possible your theory is correct." Miss Roll said excitedly. "But for that, we have to test the necklace. I will show it to you."

She opened the packet carefully and showed the most beautiful necklace the boys had ever seen. It was a diamond necklace. In each of its diamond was a circle of pure gold. In the middle was a huge ruby surrounded by ten green stones. There was a face carved on the ruby with diamonds eyes shining and below it was a broken jeweled handle.

"I see why you did not want to sell it," remarked Akash, "but it's a pity it had to be cut in two pieces. But now let's examine it."

Rohan carefully examined it inch by inch but found nothing. Finally he reached the ruby.

When he touched the left eye, he screamed in pain.

"What happened?" asked Miss Roll and Akash together.

"The diamond eye in the left was sharp and pierced in my index finger," said Rohan but could speak no more. His head was aching and he was feeling dizzy. His eyes were closed and he fell down and said, "I think th-that eye po-poisoned me." And then he fainted!

3

A Very Dangerous Case – and an Old Friend

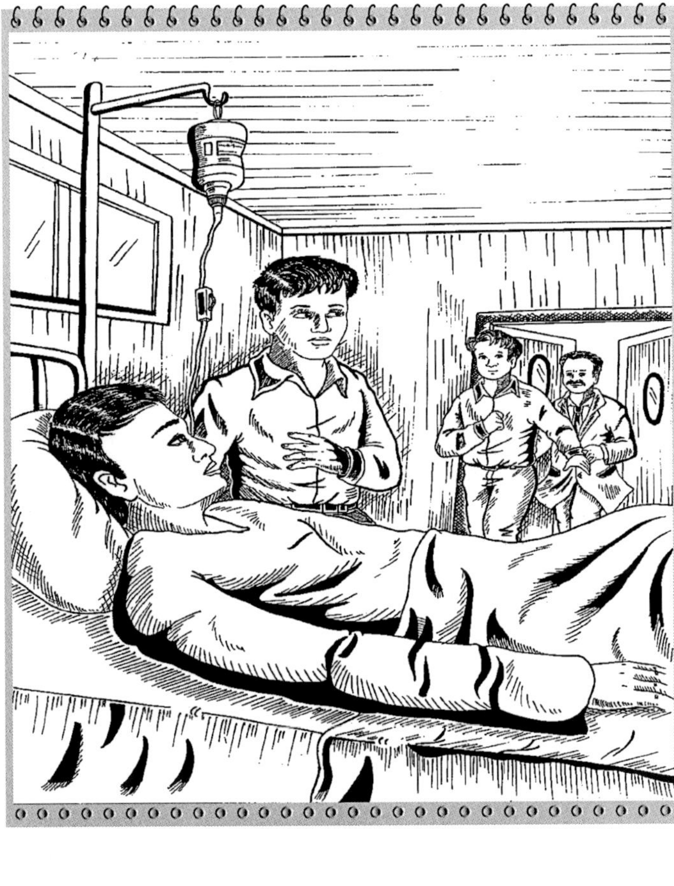

"Oh no!" said Akash terrified. His brother, poisoned! He immediately called his family doctor, Dr. Varun Gambhir. He immediately came to Miss Roll's mansion and examined Rohan. Then he said, "This venom is very harmful and dangerous. The attack is fatal. Rohan will have to be hospitalized for a week."

"What?"

"Yes."

"But a week is too much."

"I know but this is a very fatal attack," said the doctor, "but I assure you that Rohan will be all right." He telephoned for an ambulance and Rohan was taken to the hospital.

"This is entirely my fault," said Miss Roll. "I should not have shown this to you and Rohan."

"Now don't blame yourself. Rohan will be alright," Akash assured though he was also worried.

A week passed uneventfully but quickly. Everyday Akash went to Miss Roll's house to examine the necklace hoping for a good result but in vain. On the seventh day Miss Roll said, "I fear that those thieves may come again so, for safekeeping I am giving this to you. I know it would get stolen if it remains with me.

"But how can I?"

"No buts."

"Oh! Ok. I assure you I will do my best, "said Akash and went to the hospital. When he reached his brother's ward, he was happy to see that Rohan had just stirred up from his 'long sleep.' He helped him to sit and told everything that happened during his absence.

"Thank God! Nothing exciting happened else I would have missed it," said Rohan sighing deeply. "By the way, do you know what? I think I found the secret of the heirloom. Just one minute, let me think." said Rohan again.

"No need to think now, child," Said a deep, bold voice.

"Father!" Rohan said, pleased and surprised to see another figure appearing behind the inspector.

"Amir! You too?" Akash and Rohan said together.

Amir Singhania, a stout, cute boy, was on old friend of Akash and Rohan.

"Hello everyone," he boomed. "Yeah Rohan! No need to think now. Doctor has discharged you but said that you must rest for a couple of days and you should not take too much stress. By the way, is any one going to tell me anything about that mystery of yours?"

"Of course Amir."

"Don't push me in it," said Amir jokingly.

After Akash narrated all the happenings, Amar Malhotra said, "Sons, though I know you can handle this mystery, I must warn about dangers which are going to come."

"Don't worry sir, I will take care of them," joked Amir and saluted. Then he suddenly said, "Hey guys, I just had a brainwave, by which we might get forward in the case. Can you ask Miss Roll by which state's dockyard did her brother land?"

"Of course! Of course! We can get information from that dockyard and can get some good results," said Akash. "Thanks for the help Amir. Your brainwave helped us a lot!"

4

Three Tickets for Kerala Please!

Akash wanted to ask Miss Roll about the dockyard straightaway but waited so that Rohan could also go with him after a couple of days.

At last the day arrived and Akash, Rohan and Amir marched to Miss Roll's house. Amir was introduced to Miss Roll. They all sat down, Rohan came straight to the point after telling that he was all right. He asked, "Miss Roll, May I ask you a question?"

"Why not?"

Rohan told Miss Roll about Amir's plan.

"Please tell us in which dockyard did your brother go?"

"Well, now let me think, mmmmmm. Yes, got it. I think he went to Kerala in a dockyard near the famous backwaters of Allepes."

"Wow! It means we will go to Kerala. My aunt lives there. We can go and stay at her house," said Amir.

"That's good." remarked Miss Roll.

They set off to the Singhania's and waited there for five minutes because Amir went to seek permission from his parents. He returned, pleased, with his thumbs up meaning that he got the permission. The brothers were already permitted by Mr. Malhotra on the phone. As they reached their house, Akash telephoned Terminal-3 for ticket booking. The phone was answered by a clerk on the desk.

"Hello!"

"Good evening Sir! How may I help you?"

"I want three tickets for Kerala, please."

"Which airlines sir?"

"Indigo."

"Pardon sir."

"Indigo," Akash said a bit louder

"Seats available. Name of the passengers, sir."

"Akash and Rohan Malhotra and Amir Singhania. And may I know the timings earliest in the morning?"

"Pardon sir."

"I SAID MAY I KNOW THE TIMINGS EARLIEST IN THE MORNING." shouted Akash, furiously.

"Sure sir, 6:28 am sir," said the clerk in same, calm voice.

"Thank you!" Akash said angrily and put the phone down with a thud!

Soon he cooled down and told Amir all the details. Then he and Rohan packed their bags, had dinner and slept peacefully.

5

Fun at Kerala

The next day, all the boys arrived at the airport on time and sat in their seats exactly at 6:28 am. When they landed and came out of the airport, a woman in a grey car was waving towards the boys.

"Aunt Anjana!" said Amir excitedly. "You are on time for the first time." Amir grinned broadly.

Everybody got into the car and went to Anjana's house. "Kerala is a beautiful place." Remarked Rohan impressed at the view from the house. "Let's go down for dinner."

"Wow Aunt! This is a typical Kerala Meal. I've never tasted it before." Said Amir, after eating that mouth watering dish.

"I made it specially for you. Thought you would like it."

"Like it? I love it." Amir remarked.

"Let's start."

After dinner, Aunt Anjana told Amir to help the boys unpack. Amir groaned. "No need Aunt. They can do that themselves. And, even I do have to unpack."

They unpacked and did nothing for the day, though; each of them had their minds on the mystery.

The next day they set off to enjoy and wanted to have fun. They packed their lunch in two baskets as they were going to a picnic. They rented a new boat and went to a lake. At first they swam in a lake.

"Brrrrrrr! The water is so co-co-cold," remarked Akash.

They had a lot of fun in the water. Rohan swam towards Akash and pulled him underwater very quickly and kept him there for a couple of minutes. When Akash came up, the colour of his face changed from purple to red.

"You-you wait." Akash said and swam towards Rohan.

Meanwhile, Amir was laughing, seeing all the fun antics and laughed so much that, he too, fell in water and his face, too was changing colours. They even had a race of freestyle. Amir won the race. Even he did not know how he defeated such strong swimmers but was overwhelmed. After swimming, the boys dried themselves.

"Oh God! Swimming makes me hungry everytime." Said Amir. "Let's have lunch. It's quarter to two."

So they had lunch which Amir's aunt had packed.

Then, then lay in the sun for a while. The boys took their rowboat to the famous Backwaters of Allepey.

Backwaters of Allepey were a beautiful sight. There were trees surrounding it and the water was brilliantly blue. The view was spellbinding and beyond imagination. They pushed their rowboat in the water and started sailing.

"The view is stupendous," said Rohan as he and Akash started sailing by taking one oar. "Truly magnificent."

They started rowing and looked at the sky, watched the backwater as the reflection of the sky fell on the water. The water was crystal clear and lots of rare fishes were swimming below the boat. At first they thought they were in a dream, like in paradise.

"Let's do some fishing," said Amir looking helplessly at the fishes.

"Okay! Okay! But first look at yourself. You look like a beaten fish," Akash remarked, laughing endlessly, almost falling out of the boat. Amir frowned.

They took out their fishing rods and started fishing. Half an hour passed by and the boys had collected a dozen fishes. They were happy.

"Seeing these fishes makes me hungry. Let's have tea," Amir said. So they opened a basket and started taking tea.

"I can't believe I'm having tea in a boat," said Akash, who was thoroughly enjoying himself. They were having a marvellous time. Their boat was very big so each of them sat in a comfortable position. At last they hurried back home after seeing the time suddenly. They got home just after Aunt Anjana started getting worried. They had supper and dinner together as they reached very late. They then slept and started dreaming of beaches, backwaters fishes and food.

The next morning they got up quiet late, Aunt Anjana was very cross. She said, "If you don't get up early from now on, you wouldn't get breakfast."

"Aunt is very particular about these matters," said Amir from the corner of his mouth while his aunt was threatening. After breakfast, they left for another destination. They were going to a hill to do sightseeing. There were huge hills from where the pleasure and fun of sight-seeing is different. They were enthusiastic.

"Thank God! We are going to reach the top of the hill in a cable car or else I couldn't have climbed on foot," said Amir with a huge sigh of relief. They went in the cable car. When they reached at the top, they looked in awe. "Wow! What a view. It's smashing," Akash said, excited.

"Yeah! It's totally out of the world. I can see very far through my binoculars."

"Let me have a go," Amir said, taking the binoculars from Rohan and then giving it to Akash. They were amused. Then they sat on grass tired. The grass was very soft. The boys lay down for some time and then after a while, they slept soundly.

Akash woke up first. He saw a crowd going somewhere. By now, Amir and Rohan were also awake. When Akash told Rohan about the crowd, Rohan replied, "Oh Yes! I forgot to tell you. There is a performance of the traditional dances in Kerala. I think they are Kathakali and Mohiniattam."

"Yes. You are right; I'd love to see those dancers perform such old and amazing dance forms," Amir remarked.

They set off with the crowd and the performance had just started when they came to the place. The dancers had started to perform. They first performed kathakali. They wore heavy costumes and a beautiful mask over them. They danced very nicely and it was unusual to see them perform. Then the performance stopped and the other dance form, Mohiniattam started. The dancers were performing a dance form quite similar to Kathakali. It was graceful. After the performance they received a loud applause.

Then everyone left and Akash said after glancing at the watch, “Come on dude's. It's about two hours before sunset. We have to go the Eravikuem National Park, don't we?”

They hurried to the cable car, went down the hill, took their car and started off to the national park. When they entered the national park, they were amused. There were many rare animals which they had never seen before. They roamed everywhere and saw all the animals.

“The most famous ones are the Bengal Tiger, Indian Leopards and Indian Elephants,”

Rohan informed. "They are found here in great number."

"Wow! Look at those white baby elephants. They look so wonderful," Amir said.

When they started for the car, they saw a man quite familiar to them. They thought and thought and then Rohan whispered, "I know him very well. He is one of the men who tried to steal the heirloom. Let's follow him!"

6

Mysterious and Disappointing

They went off in their car and started trailing the man. He first went near a bridge and then started on busy roads.

"I don't think that he knows we are trailing him. There are so many cars behind." Rohan said. The man soon reached a lonely road and stopped. As he got off the car, the boys came out too. They walked noiselessly but kept him in sight. The man was walking slowly but suddenly he dashed off.

"I think he knows we are following him," cried Amir and the three boys dashed after him. He went through one off the narrow cuts on the road. When the boys reached the point where the man went, they could not see him anywhere as if he vanished in the air. Startled, the boys looked for him everywhere but could not find him.

"I think we lost him," Rohan said when they started towards the car.

They quickly reached home only to find their aunt worried. They ate dinner, said good night and went to bed.

"Beats me how the man vanished," said Akash for the hundredth time. They first called home as they had promised to do twice a week. They discussed matters with their father and then went to bed. Next day they woke up early because of Aunt Anjana's warning. They ate a hearty breakfast after which Rohan said, "Let us go to the place where that man vanished. I want to have a look there."

"Oh no. I do not want to go. I am very tired with the wild-goose chase last night," Amir said, yawning. So the two boys set off.

They didn't find the place for one hour. They instantly started searching.

"There might be a secret panel here as there are no houses or shops on this road where the thief could vanish," Akash said. So they started searching each and every brick on the road. For two and a half hours they found nothing. Then they got tired and rested a bit. Suddenly Akash and Rohan heard a humming sound. Both were startled. Neither of them could tell where the voice was coming from. They strained their ears but of no use. The sound stopped as quickly as it has started. "I wonder from where the sound came," wondered Rohan. "Well, now let's go to the dockyard where the ship of Miss Simon Rolls' brother had landed. I almost forgot about that." And they went off.

When they reached the backyard, they found out that except the captain of one ship, there was no other man free. The person called out, "Jones! Jones! Come here. There are visitors to collect information."

From one of the ship, came out a man in his forties. He limped a little and walked to the boys. He kindly said, "Hello, I'm Joe Jones. What information do you want?" "Do you know Mr. Roll?" Akash asked. "Oh! So you want to find out about Mr. Roll. Well, it would be hard to find a sailor like Mr. Roll," he replied. "He was a grand sailor. You should have seen him. One of the best sailors in the world. And his son, just like him. The way those son and father could handle a ship, nobody can. But now Mr. Roll is no more and goodness knows the whereabouts of Sidney."

"Sidney! Is the name of Mr. Roll's son; Sidney?" Rohan asked. "Where is he now?" "Well nobody has seen him. He is my pal and tells me everything. Something serious has happened to him. I can bet that." And the conversation ended.

The boys discussed this subject at home with Amir endlessly.

"How can he say that something serious has happened to Sidney Roll? Does he know where he is or is he hiding him?" Rohan fired question rapidly.

"Well we don't have the answer to any of your questions," replied Amir. "Though, that Joe certainly sounds suspicious and he must be hiding something that can help you further in the mystery or lead you to Sidney," Amir said, sounding like a detective and the conversation ended with squeals of laughter.

They decided for a night walk as it was full moon. They went to a hill and enjoyed the moon for a while. Just as they continued, Akash stopped. Amir asked, "Why have you stopped, Akash?"

"Nothing! Nothing! I just thought someone is following us," Akash replied with a nervous grin. They continued. Then suddenly Amir stopped too. When asked why, he replied, "I think Akash is right. Someone really is following us."

"Well, I don't agree but if you feel so, then let us search." Rohan said. They made a thorough search of the hill, but of no use. But then from nowhere a man opened and threw a rock at Rohan. He saw it and ducked just in time. Akash went running towards the man who had broken into run too. But Rohan called out, "No need. He got too much of a head start. You can't catch him. Let's head back home."

They went back, Amir joked, "Oh no! Where have I landed myself. A mystery with you boys! It's so dangerous. Count me out."

Everyone laughed and went to sleep.

7

A Good News and a Bad News

Akash woke up very suddenly around 4 a.m. He sat up straight and wondered what woke him up. Then he unknowingly went towards the window. He exclaimed and said, "Wow! This is the same hill where we went last night. And there is a figure walking on the hill so early. Let me check with the binoculars." He took them out, stuck them to his eyes and watched with keen interest. The figure which was walking on the hill was the same man who had thrown a rock over Rohan. "Wow! What a luck! This time I'll catch him. I would not let him go off my bounds today."

He got dressed and then went down quietly. On the staircase he missed the creaking steps just in case someone wakes up. He opened the door quietly and went out. The hill was not so far. He reached there in about ten minutes. When he reached the edge of the hill, he stopped. He heard sounds from the huge bramble bush. Then he heard soft footsteps fading away.

He peeped through the bush and exclaimed on what he saw. The same man on the hill was running away. "Oh no! I missed this chance too. Well whatever happens let me search the brambles. I may stumble upon something," saying this, he started. After making a good search, he saw an envelope hanging on the top most thorn. He excitedly took the envelope. It was printed in bold letter 'IMPORTANT.' He opened the letter and read it aloud:

Domon Mate,

I've got something important to tell but not in the letter in case it gets intercepted. So meet me on the 'TPOI' on Tuesday.

Alvin.

Akash was puzzled to read the letter. "Who are Domon Mate and Alvin? What kind of place is TPOI?" He kept thinking. He tried to think of a place with a name of TPOI but in vain. He then gave up and decided to discuss it with the other two. He set off to the house, happy to find a clue at last.

Meanwhile, Amir had woken from his bed just after Akash left. He stood up and checked the time. "Gosh! It's only four o' clock. How come I woke so early after the night's walk? I must check if Rohan and Akash are asleep or not. Though they must be." He said and went out of the room. He first checked Rohan's room. He was asleep. Then he went to Akash's room. He found him asleep too. "Just as I thought" he said, quietly.

When he was about to close the door of Akash's room, he stopped. He looked back at him. "He doesn't look as fat as he is looking from here." He went to inspect his bed. When he pulled the quilt, he gazed in surprise. Akash was not in his bed! He stared at the bed for few minutes. "Where could Akash be? Has he gone for a morning walk or something has happened to him?" Then he had an idea. If Akash had not gone far, he might spot him. He took the binoculars of Akash which were lying on his study table.

He looked through the window and spotted the hill. "For the night walk we went to this hill!" he exclaimed. He comforted himself by saying, "Akash must have spotted a clue and he must have gone to inspect it."

He sat there for a while, thinking of what might have happened to Akash. He thought of waking Rohan and discusses the matter with him. But he did not want to worry him. He was just going to sleep when the doorbell rang. He exclaimed, "Whoa! Now who is this so early?" Then he suddenly said, "Oh! He might be Akash. He must have come back. What a relief. "And he ran down the stairs as quickly as he can. When he came down he swung open the door. And then everything happened quite suddenly. A hand grabbed Amir's mouth and dragged him outside the house. Amir could tell that they were heading for a car. He shouted as loudly as he could but he knew that others could hear only muffled noises. Just when they came to the car, the men roughly pushed Amir and he went inside the car. Then they went away in it, taking away Amir.

When the noise of the car faded away, Akash came, excited with the bit of news he discovered. While entering the house, Akash did not notice a small envelope, half slid through the bottom of the door!

Till then, both Rohan and aunt Anjana were awake. "Where were you?" questioned Aunt Anjana. Akash winked at his brother and said, "Just gone for a morning stroll aunt." Rohan knew that it was not just a morning stroll and waited till Amir's aunt left for the kitchen. Then he eagerly asked Akash. "Where did you go?"

Akash narrated the whole incident to Rohan and showed him the bit of paper. Rohan read it and said. "Alvin and Domon must be some gang members. But TPOI is quite puzzling." "It might be a code." Akash suggested. "But first tell me, where is Amir?"

"Amir? Why, I haven't seen him all day," said Rohan.

"What do you mean; you haven't seen him all day?" questioned Akash, puzzled. "He could not be sleeping till now, could he be?"

"Akash! Rohan! Akash! Rohan! See what have I got," said Aunt Anjana, running towards the boys. "A letter!" said Rohan, seeing an envelope in aunt's hand, "Where did you get it?"

"Someone has slipped it under the main door," said aunt Anjana. Akash opened it and read the letter aloud for everybody to hear. It said:

"If you want your pal back safe and sound, leave the case this very moment."

There was no name to tell who sent it.

Aunt Anjana sat on a chair, sobbing after hearing the news. "Oh no! My nephew has been kidnapped. Amir has been kidnapped. I can't believe it. How can it happen? And who sent the letter?"

"It is anonymous," Akash explained. "There is no name under it. But I am sure that it was sent by the people who kidnapped Sidney Roll."

The boys comforted Aunt Anjana and assured her that they would find Amir as soon as they could.

They went to Rohan's room and discussed the matter. "I think that the kidnappers will not harm Amir because then it will be impossible for them to get away with their plans and they know it," Rohan said, thoughtfully. Akash added, "Also to know whether we have left the case or not, there must be somebody watching us all the time. We can have a look."

"Good idea," Rohan said.

So they went to search the grounds, the bushes, the trees, and even their garage, but they found nothing. They went back to Rohan's room and started thinking about the place by the name TPOI.

"Let us ask aunt Anjana," Rohan suggested. So they went to her, and when asked, she answered, "Well, I've never heard of such a place but you can check at the post office." "Thank You," said the boys and went to the local post office.

There, one man informed them, "Our boss Mr. Kulkarni is now at his home and the original file of addresses is with him. We are not allowed to show the copy to any stranger. But this order was given to us only yesterday. "Can we have his address?" Akash asked. "Sure," the man said, writing the address on a slip of paper and handing it to the boys.

They drove to the given address but were informed that Mr. Kulkarni was out and would not return to his house till tomorrow.

Disappointed, the boys returned to their home. There was nothing to do so the boys started reading the novels they brought. Each of them thought that their case had come to a dead end. They could neither help Miss Roll nor could they find their best friend. They were feeling very sad. Rohan kept flipping pages. He stopped on one page, He read the page carefully and then exclaimed, “I GOT IT!”

8

A Dangerous Adventure

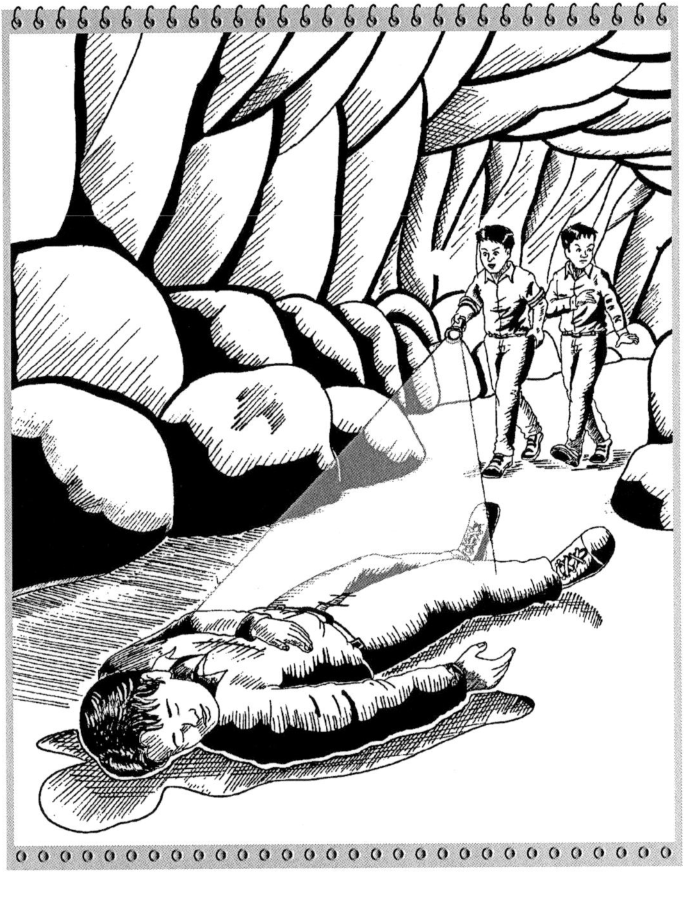

"What is the matter?" Questioned Akash, surprised by the sudden shout that came out from Rohan, "You scared me."

"I think I know what TPOI is, I can't believe it," Rohan said.

"But what is it?" said Akash now important.

"Well, TPOI is a Mulsar code." Rohan explained.

"What code?"

"Mulsar, Mulsar code. In this code the letter next to the letter which should be written is written."

By the expression on the face of Akash, Rohan understood that Akash did not understand a word he spoke. He groaned! He knew he was never good at explaining anything.

So he said, "Let's take an example. TPOI is not the real word. The real word is hmmmm. Yes! Got it! It is 'SONH.' Akash could clearly see everything. "It means the two men, Domon Mate and Alvin, or what the names were, they use letters mulsar code to communicate and there is a place called SONH where they are going to meet on Tuesday. But at what time? Time is not mentioned in the letter."

"I think it would probably be at night," Rohan said. "But I do not understand one thing, what is SONH?"

"Let's check it on district map," suggest Akash. So they brought a district map and looked at it carefully. They examined it three to four times but could not find it. They did not give up. However, they got the fruit as Aksah suddenly spotted 'SONH' on the upper left corner. Though the full form was not written, they could at last see that it is a street.

"So S stands for street," Rohan said. "If it is in the district map then Aunt Anjana might know it. She is staying here since the last seventeen years."

"I guess you are right. Let's go and ask her."

Akash along with them went off to Aunt Anjana.

"Hello Aunt," said the boys.

"Hi! Hello!"

"Aunt we need your help."

"Help! What help do you want from me?" She asked astonishingly at the boys' quest.

"Do you know any street by the short form SONH at the northern side of this area?"

"Well, let me think, yes, yes, there is one street called 'Street of no houses' or 'SONH' as you say. As the name suggests, this street is very lonely. Years ago, the Mauryan kings conquered this place and broke the houses because in these houses the men of Alexander the Great lived. Since then, the place is very spooky."

The boys were shocked at this long speech.

Certainly, Aunt has known every nook and corner of this place.

They thanked her for the information and it will be very useful. After dinner, the boys discussed about the street. “Well, if the place is as lonely as Aunt said, it would be a great place to hide Amir and it would also act as a hideout for the thieves who are after heirloom.” Akash suggested.

“Yes,” Rohan said. “I vote we keep a watch tonight as it is Tuesday tomorrow, when those two men are going to meet.”

“Agreed!”

So, as planned, the two boys spent the rest of next day thinking that what will happen that night. Time went very slowly, as though a month had passed. Finally, at 11:30 pm, they got dressed as quietly as they could and went to their car. Rohan sat on the co-passenger's seat, while Akash was behind the wheel, they reached the street without any incident. "Let's park the car away from the street."

"Right."

They then started on foot silently, under the shadow and alert. Rohan said, "Let's hide behind that wall where the bushes are. We can easily see everyone in the street without being spotted." "Good idea!" Akash commented.

They started towards the bush when they heard a sound, coming from behind them. It was coming nearer.

"Quick! Hide!" Akash said but Rohan did not need to be told twice. They both ran like wild cats and hid just when the car entered the street.

It stopped suddenly. Two men came out of it. The boys almost shouted in surprise. They were the same men who had tried to take the heirloom from Miss Roll's house. The men did not talk. It looked like they were waiting for something or someone. They were right! After a quarter of an hour, another car drew up the lane. Two men came out of it. One of the men who came earlier asked.

"Got the kid?"

"Yep."

Kid! The boys froze. Were they talking about Amir? They sat silently. One of the men came near to one of the houses. He worked out a pattern with his hands. Then the boys gasped. Part of the wall mechanically formed into a hole that widened into a tunnel. The men took out a fat boy that was surely Amir, and went inside the tunnel. After a few minutes they came back without him. "Thank God it is over," said one of the men. All of them went away in their cars.

"We must save Amir!" cried Akash.

"Yes," Rohan said, "I observed the man who was opening the tunnel. I think I remember the pattern. If we can get inside, Amir will be saved."

The boys went near the wall. Rohan tried the pattern where the tunnel had opened before. Nothing happened. He tried more times. Still nothing happened, he gave up. "I am not able to open the tunnel. We cannot save him." He kicked the wall but got hurt. Suddenly, a rumbling sound came from the wall. The tunnel was opening. "Wow! so the men touched the lowest brick and we were searching for the pattern for ages. Rohan exclaimed. The tunnel was very deep and pitch dark. "Good thing, we have our torches with us."

They started their journey. Only one torch was switched on at a time in case they had to go very far. For a long time the journey continued. At times they reach a dead end but they were determined to save Amir. They suddenly came to an attic. They were surprise to see an attic in a cave! They opened the door quietly. They saw Amir was lying there! He had been duped! Rohan found a glass of water at one corner of the room. He sprinkled few water droplets on Amir's face. Then he suddenly got up. He exclaimed! "Where am I?" Akash said, "You were kidnapped and duped. But now we must get out from here. The men might come here any time."

Rohan asked Amir, "Can you get up?"

"Yes, of course I can. They duped me but I'm fine."

"Okay, now tell me how you got stuck in here?" Akash asked.

"Well, I just woke up in my bedroom at about four O'clock, I suddenly saw that your bedroom was empty. I knew Rohan was sleeping and Aunt doesn't go out in the morning. So I decided to investigate. When I came down, everything was all right. Then suddenly someone grabbed my mouth and shoved me into a car and took me away. After that they blacked me out and that is all.

Akash said, "Well I went after the man who threw a stone towards Rohan that night and found a note." Then Akash told everything to Amir that had happened since his absence.

When it was over, the three boys heard footsteps heading their way. Rohan said, "Quick. There is no time for a talk. The guys must have heard you Amir, when you exclaimed. They must be nearing us. Let's go."

They went to the opposite tunnel. Then they went right, then left and came to a crossway. Rohan saw light in his right and signaled others to move there.

Suddenly the boys heard gunshots. They ducked. When the noise was over, they continued. Rohan said, quick. There's an opening there. Let's go. They heard more gunshots and hid behind a rock. The men came there. One of them said, "We need to find the boy or boss won't leave us.' They started for a tunnel and disappeared.

The boys gave a sigh of relief. Amir said, 'Boy, that was closed.' They reached the entrance. Rohan and Akash had the same thought in mind. They had come here before. Amir asked, 'Where are we?'

9

Cave on the Dock – and the Secret of the Heirloom

‘I think I know,' Akash said. 'We're on the same dockyard on which we went to look for Miss Roll's brother.'

Amir exclaimed, 'Oh! Is it? But why is the cave camouflaged. The people on the ships cannot see a rock from here,' he was perfectly true. The cave was well hidden by coconut and palm trees.

“But why does somebody want to hide the cave. I see that these are fake trees. Is it normal for caves on islands and dockyard?” Rohan questioned.

“I think someone does not want people to find this cave. It needs investigation,” said Akash.

“I think you're right.” Rohan said. 'It seems as someone is hiding something in the cave.'

Amir said, 'Maybe some stolen goods or stolen jewels or even...'

'A man!' exclaimed Rohan.

'A man? Do you mean Miss Roll's brother could be hidden here?'

'Yes, he could be, said Rohan.'

'If so, let's go there and check.' Amir said and started to go inside but Rohan stopped him. 'You know there are three men there with guns. If we go now and get hurt, and captured too, how could we help Miss Roll.'

'But we saw that they ran out of bullets," Amir argued.

"Though we know they don't have any more bullets or weapons," Rohan said.

"Yes," Akash told Amir, "Rohan is right. We must act fast and make some plans."

"But first we have to make sure of what's in there, or who?" Rohan said, rather sensibly. "For now let's go home. It is late and Aunt must be wondering that where are we."

They headed home. When they reached there, they found Aunt Anjana rather worried. But Amir's appearance worked like a charm. When she saw Amir, She forgot all her worries and said, "Oh Amir, I've been really worried about you. Were you kidnapped? Who kidnapped you? Why were you kidnapped? Where were you taken? Did anything happen to you?"

"Aunt, calm down, I'm back. That's all that matters, isn't it?" Amir said.

The boys grinned broadly. Sometimes elders are so fussy. They all shared some happy moments and then went to bed.

They woke up the next morning, had a quick breakfast and packed a bag with flashlights and some lunch and then set off to the cave from where they came yesterday. "Be as quiet as you can in the cave. If the men are guarding the cave even today, we might get caught." said Rohan as they reached the dockyard.

They had difficulty in finding the cave even though they had been there before as it was covered brilliantly. At last they found it and switched on their flashlights. Amir suggested that only one should be switched. But, Akash said, "No, this cave is very dark. We need more than one flashlight."

They went inside. They roamed in for what seemed like hours. Amir said tiredly, 'Oh wait, I am so tired. Let's sit down and have some food.'

Good idea.

They sat down and had a hearty lunch of a mashed potato sandwich, bread butter, and eggs.

'Wow, nothing better than having a nice, hearty lunch in a cave under the flashlights,' Amir joked.

'Let's continue to search.' They went on for some more time and then Rohan said, 'We couldn't find anything. My battery is dying out. We must go out of the cave.'

They started their way to the east and were just a bit away when their flashlights went out. 'Now what?' asked Amir, panic stricken. "I have an idea." said Akash. "I see there is some dry firewood here probably meant for the men. I brought a match box with me, just in case, you know. Let's make torches out of them."

"Good brain wave." Rohan said to his younger brother.

They made some good torches in two minutes, and then set off again. They reached the exit and blew off their torches. Then went back home. They sat in Rohan's room and discussed the matter. Akash said, "I think that the cave is just an ordinary one. Nothing suspicious."

"No," Rohan told him. "You're forgetting all the things. The men shooting, the fake trees, and even the street from where it was just a tunnel."

"But they just don't want anyone spotting them. They need privacy and peace."

"But why?" Rohan asked. "Why do they need privacy? There's a reason, they are hiding something. And I'm going to find it."

They all woke up next morning and Akash said, "Rohan, let's go to the dock. I just feel that Joe Jones knows something about this. Do you remember him? The sailor?"

"Yes we do." Both of them said together. They set off for the dock, smiling at the thoughts of their so many visits to the dockyard.

They found Joe Jones at the same place, smoking a long pipe. The boys said "hello" and he responded, "What do you want?" this time he sounded as though he wanted them all to go.

"We just want to know if there are any caves in this dockyard." Akash volunteered to ask as it was his idea.

The sailor suddenly looked nervous and angry, as if some secret was spilled out. "Caves?" He said angrily. "No, there are no caves here. You understand. No caves."

"Well, ok, if you say so, but-" Rohan started.

"I SAID NO CAVES. UNDERSTAND? CLEAR OFF, YOU THREE AND NEVER COME AGAIN, UNDERSTAND? GET OFF NOW." Joe shouted. The boys were surprised. They had never seen him so angry. Probably he knew that there were caves there and the secret was out. So he wanted to scare them off. They went quietly, as they thought that he might become wild and violent if they stayed there anymore.

At home they discussed the matter. Rohan said, "I don't understand why the sailor Joe

Jones got so angry on us. He was all right when we first saw him."

"He might be in contact with the gang of Sid Roll's kidnappers. And I suppose he knows why we are here. We discussed it last time with him, right?" Akash said,

"Yes, I think he is a bad sort of person." Amir added. Because of the discussion, the boys forgot to come down for lunch. They came down here minutes late and got a scolding from Aunt Anjana. "Boys we have to be careful now." Amir said.

They went in their room. Akash wanted to see the view from the window. He looked for his binoculars. It's nowhere. "Oh! I had kept it in the room's safe." he thought. He opened his safe and took at the binoculars. His eyes fell upon the heirloom of the Roll's family.

"Oh! I had completely forgotten about that," he exclaimed. "I have a good mind to examine it again."

He picked it up gently and went to his study room but he tripped over the corner of a chair and fell down. The heirloom was fine, though it was a few inches away from Akash.

The loud crash brought the two boys towards Akash. Rohan picked the heirloom. Amir's eyes roamed on the floor for something that fell from the heirloom, when he saw a very tiny key lying on the floor. "Hey, what's that key lying on the floor? And look, it's so small." he said.

"Where did that come from?" Akash asked. "Probably from the heirloom." Rohan said excitedly. "I think we have got the key to the secret of the heirloom."

He picked the key and searched for a key hole. He found it on a ruby. He inserted the key into it hurriedly, thinking what would come out. He turned the key and then opened a bit where the keyhole was.

They waited anxiously. Nothing happened. Rohan shaked the necklace a bit and to their immense surprise, a piece of a paper fell on the ground. Then, another piece of a thinner paper flew out on the ground.

"What could be there on the pieces of paper?" Amir asked, stunned.

"Don't know. But something very important for sure." said Rohan. He picked both the pieces and the boys went to the study.

He picked the first piece and opened it. There was a picture! 'A picture!' Amir said, astonished. The picture was of some palm and coconut trees. Then he kept the picture safely in his pocket.

Then Rohan opened the second one. He found that it was a map!

10

Searching for the Trees and a Treasure Map

"I just don't understand what it means." said Akash, frustrated. "A picture and a map! Does that make any sense? How in the world can we find its meaning?"

"I think it's something that shows us the way to some treasure, some stolen goods. There is some connection between the two things." Rohan said. His brilliant mind was racing. "The map is new to me. But the palm and coconut tress certainly ring a bell."

Then the dinner bell rang and Amir laughed saying, "the bell you heard was different, though the dinner bell rang, we should go down before we get any more scolding."

They had a good dinner and were going to bed when. Rohan said, "You guys sleep, I want to study the map and the picture." Saying this, he went to the study room and opened the map and the picture. He saw the tiny lines and the strange Spanish words. He knew little Spanish, not enough to know what is written. But he knew what to do the next day. The boys would go to a map expert and could ask him to translate the map to him. With these thoughts he slowly closed his eyes and with nice dreams he slept peacefully. He woke up around one o'clock that night when he heard the main door click.

He wondered what had happened. Had someone come in the house? What if a burglar? He might've seen the key under the door mattress. He got up from the chair and silently came to the corridor. He saw that the burglar was the same person who broke in Miss Roll's house in Gurgaon!

He also saw that he was trying to open the safe. He must not take the heirloom. Swiftly, but silently, Rohan walked behind and jumped at him. But the burglar recovered quickly and punched Rohan. He ducked and threw a few rabbit punches in his stomach. The man stumbled and fell on the floor. Rohan took a rope and tied the man while the noise woke everyone in the house, Amir, Akash and Aunt Anjana. She asked Rohan what had happened. Rohan explained the incident then turned towards the man.

"We were not able to send you and your pal to jail in Gurgaon so you came after us to Kerala. Looks as if you want to experience life in prison. But first, tell me, did you come to steal the heirloom?"

"Heirloom? What Heirloom? I don't know any Heirloom." the man said.

"Oh don't try to fool us. It would not be of any use." Rohan argued.

"I won't say anything." said the man, angrily.

"Okay then. Call the cops, Akash. They'll teach him a lesson." Rohan said. The cops arrived, thanked Rohan for catching the thief and took him away. "What a night!" Aunt Anjana said, "I'll make some hot tea for you all and then we can go back to sleep."

The next day Rohan asked Aunt Anjana for a map expert. "Yes. I happen to know one." She replied, thinking deeply. "He is my brother's friend. His name is Karan Khurana. Here is the address." She wrote it on a piece of paper and gave it to him. Akash and Amir asked Rohan why had he wanted the map expert's address.

He told them, "I will take the map of Heirloom to him and as the words are written in Spanish; he can translate and draw the map on this A-4 size sheet. It would be much clear then."

The others liked his idea and they set off to the shop which looked like an ancient one. They went inside and found that, it was a dusty shop with all kinds of maps present. A middle aged person sat at the desk and looking at Amir, said in a loud voice, "Ah, you are Amir, aren't you? I played with you a lot when you were small. And you still have the chubby face of yours." Amir replied, "Hello err-uncle Karan. Meet my friends, Rohan and Akash. They want to know something about a map. A Spanish map."

"Oh, I know Spanish perfectly, I can translate the whole map for you," he said confidently. "That's what we are here for. We want you to copy this map in English on a sheet of paper I have brought," Akash said, holding the map and the sheet.

"Okay" said uncle Karan. He looked at the map closely. As though shocked, he sat up straight. The boys were surprised at his strange behavior. The man took his magnifying glass and looked at the map closely. He again sat up straight. “I can't believe it. I just can't believe it.” He said, excitedly standing up.

“You all are lucky guys. I must say” he said, turning to them.

“But why?” Akash asked.

“The words printed here are, 'Mapa Del Teroso,' which means a treasure map!” Karan said.

“What?” Amir asked, jumping continuously. “Is it really a treasure map? Is-is it genuine?”

“Yes, it is.” said Karan.

“But we still don't know from where to start with,” said Rohan.

“It has to be started from the place in the picture,” Akash said, his eyes gleaming.

Rohan turned to the shopkeeper and said. “Can you translate the map in English on this sheet of paper for us?”

"Certainly."

The boys took the real map and its copy, thanked the shop owner and left.

"Well, now that we have come here, let's visit the dockyard; though quietly in case Joe Jones spots us," Akash suggested.

"Agreed," said the other two.

They went to the highway and then came to the dockyard. They wandered quietly for a while, watching the ships being filled with lots of things and the passengers boarding their chosen ships.

Amir was very excited to see such beautiful freight ships. First his eyes looked at the ships, large and beautiful they were. But suddenly he looked at the cave entrance. He examined the entrance closely for a while that behaved very weirdly, by moving right, then left, then right again. Akash and Rohan asked together.

'What happened Amir?'

'Guys I think I've spotted the trace of the heirloom,' said Amir.

11

Inside the Cave

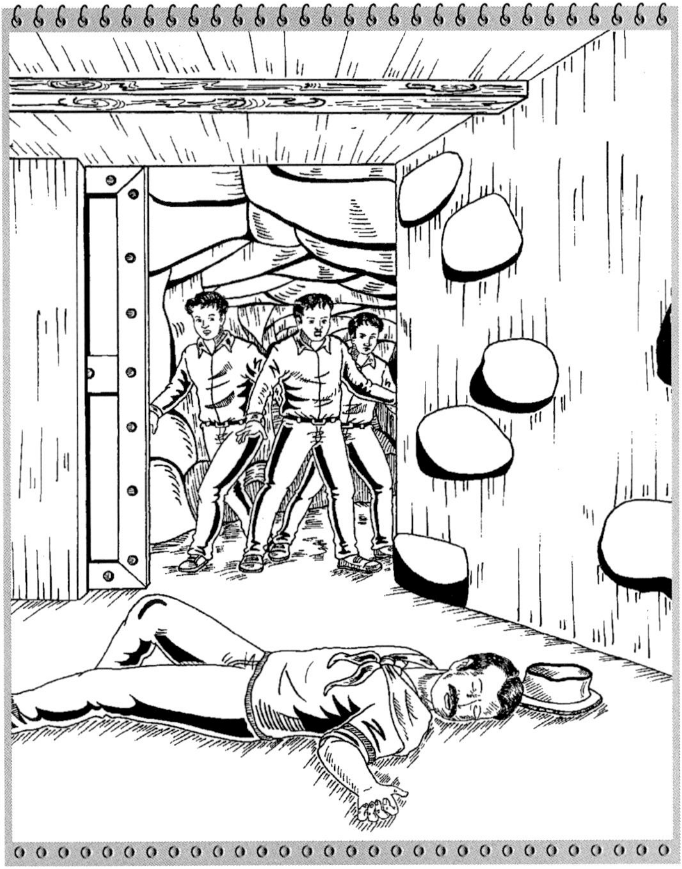

"What? Where?" Akash asked.

"The trees which are covering the cave." Amir said, pointing out proudly.

"Why didn't we think of that? These trees should have been our first suspicion." Rohan said. "Today we'll go home and plan everything. Then at night we'll come and explore the cave around fifteen to twelve."

The plans they made were too many. Akash said, "This time we'll take extra batteries with us."

"I think that we should take some food too. Exploring is hard work, guys." Amir said.

"And we'll take no maps or picture. We will memorize the maps so that if we are caught, our captor won't take the map and get the treasure." said Rohan.

"Sometimes I take pity on your brain." Amir told Rohan.

"It works so hard."

The other's laughed. Rohan took out his map and displayed it. They memorized and put it in a drawer. "Now I just wish tonight would come soon." Akash said, but he did not know what problems he would have to face.

The day was uneventful. It went smoothly. The boys always kept talking about the cave. They were excited to know what would happen that night. Aunt Anjana was surprised to see the strange behavior. She questioned them several times but they did not tell her.

At eleven o'clock everyone went to do some work in fear of sleeping. Akash read books, Rohan made all the preparations, food, flashlights and a bag with first-aid kit. Yes, everything was ready. Then he sat on the sofa and started reading a book.

Soon the clock striked- 11:45. The boys got ready to go. They went quietly down the stairs and to the main door so as not to disturb Aunt Anjana.

They went up to the drive and with Akash behind the wheel, they went off. They routed the dockyard in fifteen minutes; usually it took them half an hour's time but as there were no vehicular traffic they reached quickly. They reached the cave quietly without disturbing the men sleeping in the ships. They switched on their flashlights and started their journey inside the cave.

As per the map, they first came across a place where they had to turn right. Then they went on and on for at least half a mile. Then turned right again, another walk for 800 meter. Then Amir said, "Guys, I am tired. Let's stop for a healthy picnic. We can sit under that cool shade."

They went there and had a good picnic, though nobody said a word. It was quite strange. Usually picnics are done in bright pleasant spots, where everyone keeps on chattering, with nothing to worry about. But now they were in a pitch dark cave, solemn and quite, and worried about being kidnapped or even worse than that.

"Let's keep the mattress and utensils under that rock and I expect they would be safe. This way we could roam around the cave easily, without any load." Said Akash and they continued their journey. They took one right turn and came to a very narrow tunnel which was wide from up. There were poles over there by which they could cross the tunnel. "Now here is the rough part," said Rohan.

They managed to cross the tunnel after some time by holding the flashlights in their mouth. They then reached a door. It was unlocked. Rohan whispered, "Keep quiet. Let me go in and see. If everything is okay, I will call you."

He went inside. There were about eighteen men sleeping and there was an attic door. He gestured Akash and Amir to come in and they slowly went to the attic door. It was bolted from outside. They went in and found a man inside, lying unconscious. Amir said, "Oh! He must be Sidney Roll."

The boys shook the man. Then he stirred and opened his eyes. He sat up shaking. "Are you Sidney Roll?" Amir asked.

"Ye-Yes, I am. But how d-do you kn-know me?"

Akash and Rohan told the whole story, interrupted by Amir sometimes. When they finished, Rohan asked, "But how did you end up-here?"

Sidney told his story, "When I went to Spain, I found that necklace but a man named Bonagu learned about it. He also learned that my next trip was to India. Fortunately, I got away from him in Spain. But there was another great treasure about which I learned from the necklace. Bonagu's man kept an eye on me all the time but I did not know it. So he told Bonagu about the treasure. So when I reached India, he kidnapped me.'

"When I did not tell him about the treasure, he forced me to tell him about the cave. Inside he made some attics and storage rooms. He kept me there and gave me one meal and two glasses of water a day."

"Now we must leave before we get captured." Rohan said, wisely.

They all got up. Slowly but steadily, they moved on, till they came in the room when the man were sleeping. They were halfway to the room when someone said 'Stop.' The boys and Sidney looked back and there were men standing there. "You guys thought you'd get away from us, didn't you?"

Rohan said, "Attack!" and the boys threw one of the men away. Then one of them hit Amir from the back, though not so hard. Amir used one of his karate moves on which he had been practicing. He punched directly on the chin and knocked him out. Akash and Rohan took two of the men at once and fought furiously. But as more of the men got up and came to face the boys, they knew that they were outnumbered. They gave up.

'Okay guys. Now be good and go inside,' man said who seemed to be the leader of the gang.

The boys followed Sidney, who did not join the fight as he was weak. Some heavy and strong ropes tied the boys firmly. They struggled but could not loosen the ropes. The men silently went out and bolted the door. "Oh no! What have we done to earn this?" Amir said.

"We will have to think of some way now." Rohan said quite confidently, but inside he was not as confident as he sounded. After a few minutes, their feet and hands felt numb.

"Oh, it's so hot here." Akash said.

"We'll have to think of some plan soon." Rohan said, everyone started to think but nobody could. Amir said, "We can do nothing, it's all a waste. We all will die here."

They felt as though they couldn't breathe properly. Akash thought that he must do something. He was determined to save everyone and send the thieves to prison. Suddenly he said, "I have a plan!"

12

A Marvelous Plan

Meanwhile, at Aunt Anjana's house, she had woken up just half an hour after the boys had left. She had woken up to drink water. But when she reached the fridge, a couple of utensils fell on the floor and made a loud noise. She thought that the boys would have come to the kitchen. She decided to wait till they came and send them back to sleep. But nobody came. She waited for some more time. But still nobody came. She became suspicious. She went upstairs to see what they were doing. She reached Amir's room, opened it, and to her surprise Amir's bed was empty!

She calmed herself. Maybe he was in somebody else's room. She checked Akash's room and then Rohan's. But their rooms were also empty. She screamed out, "Rohan! Amir ! Akash! Where are you?"

She was scared. She thought that this time all the three boys were kidnapped. She checked the doormat. No, this time there was no note. She heavily sat down on the sofa in the living room. Oh no! The children were her responsibility. Now what answer shall I give to my brother and Mr. Malhotra?

She was sobbing on the chair but then made determined face and said, "I will not give up, I will search in every nook and corner of the house and the garden too. I must find them. I must not give up so soon."

She comforted herself a bit, and then went to the storeroom. No boys! To the drawing room no boys! To the study room and then the kitchen still no boys!

Oh no! Now she was shattered. The kidnapper might do something to the kids. What shall she do? Call the state police? No, that would be late. Yes, she would call Mr. Malhotra. He is a highly respected policeman. He would know what to do. She opened her telephone, saw his residential number and dialed it. She waited anxiously. Mrs. Malhotra took the receiver.

"Mrs Malhotra, is your husband in the house?" said Aunt Anjana.

"Well, no. But what to do?"

"Where is he?" Aunt Anjana interrupts.

"He is in Bangalore. But what happened?"

"Now is not the time to tell you. I must hurry," said Aunt Anjana and put down the phone. "Good.Bangalore is closer than Delhi. The police chief might even come here at the news of the boys disappearance."

She dialed his number. Amar Malhotra picked up the phone.

"Hello, Mr Malhotra. I'm Anjana speaking, Amir's aunt."

"Yes. What has happened? You sound scared."

"Yes, I am. Your sons and Amir has disappeared. And I need your help. You're in Bangalore. Could you come here by any chance?" said aunt Anjana.

"What? They have disappeared? I will come there in half an hour. You alert the state police and tell them that I am coming there too." The inspector said and the call ended.

The inspector drove a bit too fast, worried for Akash and Rohan. He entered Kerala and then went to Aunt Anjana's house. There he found a police van. He parked his car beside it. He entered the house and was greeted merrily by Aunt Anjana and several police officers. "Wow inspector. I never thought I would get the chance to meet you. You are very famous for your work." said a police sergeant.

"Any clues to where my sons are?" asked Amar Malhotra, calmly.

"Yes sir. We asked some people on the roads. One of them said that he heard some boys who were talking about a dockyard." said the same sergeant.

"And you know where this dockyard is?" asked Mr. Malhotra.

"Yes sir, we do have an idea. There is a dockyard on which we have been keeping watch for a long time on suspicion. But we don't have any evidence. We will search it, though," said the sergeant and they set off, except Aunt Anjana who protested but Amar Malhotra said, "This work is dangerous. The crooks want something, I am sure. They could do anything to achieve it."

"But the children were my responsibility and..." started Aunt Anjana but Amar Malhotra interrupted, "They are mine now. Leave this thing to the police, I request you. I will bring everyone safe and sound. " Saying this he and the other police officers went off.

Inside the cave, Akash told his idea to everyone, "Listen, the man with the food will come here any moment. And for us to eat, he will un-tie us. We all will put all our strength and pounce on him. Rohan, your build and height is the best compared to Bonagu's men. You will take his clothes and act like him, go outside then with some excuses and call the police. We all will be saved and the crooks will be captured. This way Sidney can have his treasure too."

Everyone looked at Akash. He thought of the best plan anyone could ever try to think of in such a difficult situation.

"Bravo." Rohan praised. "Good Idea. Though, I feel a bit nervous about acting."

"Oh come on. You did so well in the school play." Akash said.

"But this is not a school play. This is really a tough situation. Though that's the only way we can be saved, I'll do my best." Rohan promised.

Now, every one of them was silent. Will they succeed? Or they would stay here forever?

Nobody knows. Akash thought, would his plan work? If not, Rohan might even be killed. Oh! He kept thinking about it worriedly.

Rohan was making some plans himself. He would try not to walk stiffly and he also thought that he would first get out every bit of information that he could. He would have to save his friends and also help Sidney find the treasure. But what excuse could he give to go out. He wanted a bit of fresh air.

No, that wouldn't do. He could say that he wanted to do some guard duty. No, someone would be sure to come and see him. As these thoughts came into his mind, everyone heard someone pull the door and a man came in. Everyone was nervous. Rohan saw that he was wearing a cap so that nobody could see him. He was very happy with this, nobody would be able to see him. The man untied the ropes. Everyone soon found out that they could barely move.

'Quick,' said the man, harshly.

They started eating. After eating some bites, they got their energy back. They had fully recovered. Everyone was happy. Now they could easily fight with the man.

The man got up to take their plates and put it away. He came back to tie the boys and

Sidney. As he was busy tying Akash, Amir used one of his moves called sidekick and hit the man on the head. The man seemed dizzy and then Rohan punched him so hard that he was knocked out. The first stage of their plan had worked successfully though a lot of hurdles were still left to overcome.

13

Police Arrives

"Good punch." said Sidney.

"Now let's tie him but before that I will change his clothes." Rohan said.

In no time he looked exactly like the man. "Now you will learn a lesson." Rohan copied the man's same harsh voice. Everyone laughed quietly. They tied the man properly and then Rohan went out, confident of this success.

"Gave'em food, have you?"

"Yeah." said Rohan. "Where's Jones anyway? He doesn't come often, does he?" Rohan took the risk of asking about Joe Jones. Thankfully, he was correct in guessing the Joe Jones was with the gang.

"No, he doesn't," said one of them. "He is useless. Couldn't even keep those boys away from the hideout. Still, it's good that they are not an obstacle anymore. Sometimes I wonder why did boss choose Jones."

"Yeah. Not much good he is?" Rohan said.

"By the way Charlie," One of the men said, addressing to Rohan. "Did you try to talk to Sidney? He is not telling us a word."

"Yes. I tried. But as usual, he's as stiff as a stick. Says he wouldn't tell us anything about the treasure."

Suddenly, Rohan remembered the name of Domon. He did not seem to be there. So Rohan's next question was, 'Is Domon guarding the cave, I heard that he almost got caught by one of those boys.'

"Yes, he did. Very foolish of him. Good thing, boss doesn't know about it. He would have been furious with him."

"I do wonder the boys have told someone about our secret. We don't want to get caught, do we?" Rohan asked.

"Yeh, I thought about it. But they might not have told anyone as the women in their house must have forbidden it," said one of them, who was lying on his bunk.

Rohan went to the nearest bunk and sat down. "Hey, that's my bunk," said a man.

Rohan saw that there was a name 'Borego' written on the bunk he sat on. Beside was the bunk of Charlie, so he said, "Oh, my mistakes, mine is just beside it, you know. It happens sometimes." Saying this, he went to Charlie's bunk and sat on it.

He thought of what excuse to make. He might have to stay here all the time. He would have to go out. What if he couldn't help the others? And the real Charlie was inside, knocked out? But his problems were finished as someone said, "Charlie! Charlie! It's your turn to guard the cave now; Jacob has been there for four hours. Quick, go now."

Rohan was very happy. Now the crooks will get captured, but suddenly he remembered one more name, Alvin. So he said, "Why couldn't Alvin do it?"

"Because I did it earlier." said a man, who looked like Alvin, growling.

"Ok, Ok, I'm going now." Rohan pretended to be growling back, though inside, he was the happiest person in the world.

He slowly made his way back to the cave end. But he took the wrong turn! So he kept on going till he realized what had happened. "Oh no this cave is a labyrinth. I'll have to go back to the place where I took a wrong turn. I wondered why that narrow tunnel. Let's see now, hmm I will go in right then left and some more turns. Yes, this place. I seem to remember it, let's go," saying this, he kept on going when he reached the narrow tunnel. He went on, reached the picnic spot and suddenly felt hungry. He ate for a few minutes and then realised that how happy he was. He felt like the King of the world.

He continued. He then saw a man. Thinking the man must be Jacob, he called out, "Jacob! Come here. You may go now. It's my chance to guard the cave."

"Well, you're late." Jacob said. "But now that you have come, I should be going now." And he went towards the hideout.

"Now I must do something," Rohan said, but forgot that he was alone and still he was talking to himself in the same, harsh voice. He laughed. He was going outside when he heard voices. He stopped. As silently as he could, he went outside. He peered through the trees and found Joe Jones just in front of him, with a knife in hand. And he also had Amar Malhotra, with his knife pointed to him!

"Nobody will come forward unless you want your friend dead." Joe Jones was in full anger, growling like anything.

Rohan was horrified. He must do something to save his father. Then he had an idea. He would pretend to be Charlie again and do some talking and police will catch him.

So he appeared and said, “Hey Jones. What are you doing? Have you got yourself in trouble?” Rohan said.

“See what, Charlie. I've got the well known policeman out of his wits whom we were talking about.”

“Yes, I remember, Amar Malhotra you said. Well at least you are of some use.”

“What do you mean by that? I scared those boys who asked me about the cave.”

“Oh no, you didn't. Do you know what? The boys came into the cave and they were going to rescue the Roll man but thankfully, boss knew how to choose members of his gang. But he should know that he made a mistake while choosing you.” Rohan said though he did not know how he managed to say so much to a criminal.

"How dare you?" growled Joe Jones.

"With my mouth," Rohan said harshly, and gave a high pitched laugh as he had seen the real Charlie doing it.

"I will complain to boss, you just wait." Joe said.

"Oh! Leave that to me. It's good that you will confess your mistake, but it would make him ever angrier when somebody other than you complains about you." Rohan said.

Joe Jones lost himself. He dropped his knife and ran at Rohan. He tried to punch as hard as he could but Rohan ducked. He pushed Joe to Mr. Malhotra, who at once handcuffed Joe. Some police officers were coming to Rohan, but he said "Wait." in his own voice. Then he removed his cap and revealed himself.

"Rohan!" Amar Malhotra said.

"Dad. How did you get here?"

"Well, your aunt learned about your disappearance and called me for help. I came here, and we questioned some men. One of them heard you when you were talking about this dockyard. So we came here at once. But how come you are up here? And where are the others?"

Rohan explained all the events and also about Akash's plan. Then he said, "By now the men must have realized about my disappearance. If we don't hurry, they would escape. I vote that we have to go in."

"Yes, we should," the sergeant-in charge said. "Officer Rao, Officer Kabir you keep watch on this Joe Jones incase he runs away. Till then, we'll go and arrest the other men."

"I'll lead the way." Rohan added.

The team went inside the cave. They thought that it was weird. One of the constable said, "I have never even seen such a thing in my life although I have been a constable of this area since ten years. They continued as silently as they could, they went towards the thieves and their hideout. They felt that even their breathing would alert the thieves and create havoc.

They entered the hideout. Then Amar Malhotra said loud and clear, "Your game is up."

14

Secrets Spill Out

Every thief ran in a different directions. The police had tracked them down, and this was the best place they could hide in. They were terrified. The police ran here and there to catch the thieves. Seeing such a chaos, one of them tried to get away. Rohan saw this and threw a small stone at his legs. He fell down and Rohan took a handcuff from a policeman and then put it on the thief. One policeman went to a room and saved all the others. Now every criminal was rounded up. They all answered to each of them truthfully, scared. Rohan asked Alvin, "Are there some other men with you all?"

"What's that to do with you?" He said.

"Are you speaking or not?" Akash said, very angrily at his captors.

"But can't you see that we are all here."

"I'm waiting for a proper answer." Rohan said, looking at his clock, in a funny manner.

"Search for yourself." The man sniggered.

Two policemen went in and came out with a man.

"Who's he?" Amar Malhotra asked.

"Our cook."

"He looks innocent. But we'll keep him for some questioning." Said the sergeant.

"Who is your boss?" Amar Malhotra asked.

"A man named Bonagu." Akash said.

"I will call the headquarters to send his picture if he has had any records," the sergeant said, taking his phone out of his pocket. He spoke on the phone, "Officer Singh, we want to trace down a foreign criminal that might be in Kerala now. He is called Bonagu. Please check if he has any records and send a picture of him soon."

"Now can I-I g-go?" the cook said, after having answered a dozen questions.

"Yes, you can," Amar Malhotra released the cook. "Now it's time we take prisoners to their new hideout, the jail."

As they started leaving, they heard a phone ringing. One of the criminals slowly took the phone out, trembling.

"Who is calling you?" one constable demanded.

"Bo-Boss." He said.

"Talk to him. Put the phone on speaker."

The man did as he was told. He spoke, "Yes Boss."

"Don't try to fool me. I think you all are fools. Why did I choose such a bunch of idiots in my gang in the first place?" Bonagu had an angry, high pitched voice. A chill ran down the thief's spine.

"What is the matter Boss?" he asked.

"What is the matter!" said Bonagu. "You all are standing in front of police and asking me what is the matter? You all have let me down. A couple of boys are much more clever than you all."

The thieves shivered. The police was surprised. How came Bonagu knows that the thieves, his team members are captured.

"How do you know all this, boss?" asked the man.

"Oh never mind. Even if I tell you, nothing would go inside your lousy head." Bonagu said, angrier than ever after being asked a questioned by one of this gang members. "Give a message to the police. Even if I am alone, I am strong and much cleverer. Nobody could catch me. They would tire their strength and brain while doing so. And listen, you Amar Malhotra. You have solved every case given to you. But this will be your first failure. Get this thing inside your head." There was a sound of click on the other side of the phone and the call ended.

For a few minutes everyone kept wondering that how come Bonagu got to know about this incident? Rohan asked the man named Borego.

"Do you know where Bonagu is now?"

"No. Because wherever he was he would run from there."

"How does Bonagu look like?" Akash asked.

"I don't know." said Borego.

"What do you mean you don't know? Have you not seen him?"

'No. None of us have."

"Then why are you working for him?'"Asked the sergeant.

"Because he threatened our lives." Borego said.

Suddenly, the Sergeant's phone started ringing.

"Maybe, the picture has come." The sergeant took out his phone. He saw the picture. "I think I know who he is." The sergeant said, straining his mind. Rohan and the other boys looked at the picture. Amir suddenly exclaimed and said, "I know who he is! I know who he is! He is the cook who we thought was innocent." The other's looked at it and said "Yes you are right."

"We should go and catch him before he gets away." Rohan said.

So Rohan, Akash, Amir, Amar Malhotra, and the sergeant went towards the criminal. The other policemen and Sidney stayed with the rest of the prisoners. When they were running towards the exit, Akash saw a running figure. "Over there," he whispered.

They soon caught up with the villain. Akash pulled him down with a flying tackle but he was strong. He put up a good fight. But then Rohan and Amir joined the fight and that guy was helpless.

"Okay. Now get up from me. I surrender." he said.

"So. You put up a good disguise. Specially your voice. None of your fellows knew that you were their cook." Rohan said.

"Yeah. I told you before. They all are fools. I always called Borego from the kitchen and he didn't know it was me." Bonagu said.

"You thought you are clever, didn't you?" Amar Malhotra said. "You thought that you could defeat me. But these three boys would not let you."

Now they took all the thieves to the police station.

"I want to sleep now." said Akash.

"But Sidney! Where will you go?"

"I don't know."

"Why don't you come to our house?" Akash said.

"But-but."

"No buts. You're coming and that's final."

Akash said. "Then when we get up, we all will go to look for your treasure."

"Okay, if you say so." Sidney said.

So, they went to their homes and explained to Aunt Anjana about Sidney's arrival. They slept around 4:30 am. They woke late in the afternoon, (But this time Aunt Anjana did not scold them.) and started towards the cave.

Soon they came to the big room in which they all were held as captives. Sidney went to a statue and to the boys' astonishment; he moved the head of the statue!

Suddenly, the wall behind the statue gave a low rumble and gave way to another room. They entered there and saw such things which were out of this world!

There were necklace, pots, finely carved utensils, rings, daggers and many other things. "You all sailors are lucky." Amir said "This may become my profession after I finish my studies."

Akash and Rohan were eager to find out whether they might have another case to solve. This one came to them by chance. But their worries were no more. They had enjoyed this case. What more did they want? They were even successful. Akash then said, "All's well that ends well!"